Jemima the Spy

Level 4G

Written by Melanie Hamm
Illustrated by Lawrence Chase

What is synthetic phonics?

Synthetic phonics teaches children to recognise the sounds of letters and to blend (synthesise) them together to make whole words.

Understanding sound/letter relationships gives children the confidence and ability to read unfamiliar words, without having to rely on memory or guesswork; this helps them to progress towards independent reading.

Did you know? Spoken English uses more than 40 speech sounds. Each sound is called a *phoneme*. Some phonemes relate to a single letter (d-o-g) and others to combinations of letters (sh-ar-p). When a phoneme is written down it is called a *grapheme*. Teaching these sounds, matching them to their written form and sounding out words for reading is the basis of synthetic phonics.

Consultant

I love reading phonics has been created in consultation with language expert Abigail Steel. She has a background in teaching and teacher training and is a respected expert in the field of synthetic phonics. Abigail Steel is a regular contributor to educational publications. Her international education consultancy supports parents and teachers in the promotion of literacy skills.

Reading tips

 This book focuses on the igh sound, made with the letters i and y, as in find and sky.

Tricky words in this book

Any words in bold may have unusual spellings or are new and have not yet been introduced.

Tricky words in this book:

favourite said straight climbing audience leapt where curtain awry

Extra ways to have fun with this book

After the reader has read the story, ask them questions about what they have just read:

Who was the kidnapper?

Where did Jemima look for Linus?

Hi boys and girls!
I'm Simon Sly!

A pronunciation guide

This grid contains the sounds used in the stories in levels 4, 5 and 6 and a guide on how to say them. /a/ represents the sounds made, rather than the letters in a word.

/ai/ as in game	/ai/ as in play/they	/ee/ as in leaf/these	/ee/ as in he
/igh/ as in kite/light	/igh/ as in find/sky	/oa/ as in home	/oa/ as in snow
/oa/ as in cold	/y+oo/ as in cube/music/new	long /oo/ as in flute/crew/blue	/oi/ as in boy
/er/ as in bird/hurt	/or/ as in snore/oar/door	/or/ as in dawn/sauce/walk	/e/ as in head
/e/ as in said/any	/ou/ as in cow	/u/ as in touch	/air/ as in hare/bear/there
/eer/ as in deer/here/cashier	/t/ as in tripped/skipped	/d/ as in rained	/j/ as in gent/gin/gym
/j/ as in barge/hedge	/s/ as in cent/circus/cyst	/s/ as in prince	/s/ as in house
/ch/ as in itch/catch	/w/ as in white	/h/ as in who	/r/ as in write/rhino

Sounds this story focuses on are highlighted in the grid.

/f/ as in phone	**/f/** as in rough	**/ul/** as in pencil/ hospital	**/z/** as in fries/ cheese/breeze
/n/ as in knot/ gnome/engine	**/m/** as in welcome /thumb/column	**/g/** as in guitar/ghost	**/zh/** as in vision/beige
/k/ as in chord	**/k/** as in plaque/ bouquet	**/nk/** as in uncle	**/ks/** as in box/books/ ducks/cakes
/a/ and **/o/** as in hat/what	**/e/** and **/ee/** as in bed/he	**/i/** and **/igh/** as in fin/find	**/o/** and **/oa/** as in hot/cold
/u/ and short **/oo/** as in but/put	**/ee/**, **/e/** and **/ai/** as in eat/ bread/break	**/igh/**, **/ee/** and **/e/** as in tie/field/friend	**/ou/** and **/oa/** as in cow/blow
/ou/, **/oa/** and **/oo/** as in out/ shoulder/could	**/i/** and **/ai/** as in money/they	**/c/** and **/s/** as in cat/cent	**/y/**, **/igh/** and **/i/** as in yes/sky/myth
/g/ and **/j/** as in got/giant	**/ch/**, **/c/** and / **sh/** as in chin/ school/chef	**/er/**, **/air/** and **/eer/** as in earth/bear/ears	**/u/**, **/ou/** and **/oa/** as in plough/dough

> Be careful not to add an 'uh' sound to 's', 't', 'p',
> 'c', 'h', 'r', 'm', 'd', 'g', 'l', 'f' and 'b'. For example,
> say 'fff' not 'fuh' and 'sss' not 'suh'.

Every evening Jemima Bind liked to unwind with her **favourite** show, "Find Me An Idol".

It was presented by
Linus Likable, the liveliest,
smiliest TV star.

But as Jemima was lying in bed
that night, her mobile rang.
It was Agent Mindful.

He **said**, "Jemima, you are required at Spy HQ. Linus Likable has been kidnapped!"

Jemima biked **straight** to
Spy HQ. "We're relying on you!"
cried Agent Mindful.

"Find Linus Likable... and discover who is behind this crime!"

Jemima realised the
kidnapper was wily.

She tried hiding in a
grimy alley. No Linus.

She tried **climbing** a shiny skyscraper.

No Linus.
But then she had an idea...

Tonight was the final of
"Find Me An Idol".

Jemima filed in behind the studio
audience.
Quietly she bided her time.

Soon the title music chimed.
But the audience were surprised
for onto the stage **leapt**...

Simon Sly!
"**Where** is Linus Likable?"
they cried.

"Kidnapped by this slimy fly!"
replied Jemima.

"I deny it!" lied Simon Sly.
But behind the **curtain** was
Linus, tied up!

Jemima untied him. The audience
went wild! Linus stepped up to
the mic. "Her name is Bind,
Jemima Bind — and she's the

finest spy there is!"
As for Simon Sly, he suddenly
seemed shy. Everything had
gone **awry** – even his wig!

OVER **48** TITLES IN SIX LEVELS
Abigail Steel recommends...

Other titles to enjoy from Level 4

I love reading phonics — **The Circus Mice** — 978-1-84898-582-7

I love reading phonics — Monster's **Night** — 978-1-84898-583-4

I love reading phonics — **The Mummy Code** — 978-1-84898-585-8

Some titles from Level 5

I love reading phonics — **The Gigantic Bear** — 978-1-84898-586-5

I love reading phonics — **Celebrity Celia** — 978-1-84898-587-2

I love reading phonics — **The Cemetery Dance** — 978-1-84898-588-9

Some titles from Level 6

I love reading phonics — **Hugh is New** — 978-1-84898-590-2

I love reading phonics — **Clumsy Eagle** — 978-1-84898-591-9

I love reading phonics — **Bad Zombie Movie** — 978-1-84898-592-6

An Hachette UK Company
www.hachette.co.uk

Copyright © Octopus Publishing Group Ltd 2012
First published in Great Britain in 2012 by TickTock, an imprint of Octopus Publishing Group Ltd,
Endeavour House, 189 Shaftesbury Avenue, London WC2H 8JY.
www.octopusbooks.co.uk

ISBN 978 1 84898 584 1

Printed and bound in China
10 9 8 7 6 5 4 3 2 1